1946

1946

# Adalbert Stifter

# ROCK CRYSTAL

### A CHRISTMAS TALE

*Rendered into English by*
*Elizabeth Mayer and Marianne Moore*
*Illustrations by Josef Scharl*

PANTHEON BOOKS

## PUBLISHER'S NOTE

*It is exactly 100 years ago that this story was first pub-*
*lished as a "Christmas offering," under the title* HOLY
EVE. *Later, Stifter rewrote it and incorporated it in a col-*
*lection of short stories which he called "Colored Stones"*
(BUNTE STEINE). *As each tale in this collection is*
*named after some mineral or semiprecious stone which*
*stands as a symbol for the character of the story,* HOLY
EVE *was renamed* ROCK CRYSTAL, *and the scrupulous*
*author commented: "Were I permitted to polish and reset*
*this tale a third time, by the powers of heaven I believe it*
*might become a diamond."*

*Stifter was born at Oberplan in Bohemia in 1805 and*
*died in 1868. His work, admirable for its pure and beautiful*
*prose, its loving and true description of nature, was counted*
*by Nietzsche among the rare examples of German writing*
*which deserved to be read again and again; "Here still lies*
*a whole world of beauty."*

*A fervent admirer of Goethe and himself a true classicist,*
*Stifter loved order and exactitude and was given to a pains-*
*taking truthfulness which some modern readers may find*
*irksome. To condense and prune his prose was a temptation*
*to be resisted out of respect for an author who did not write*
*lightly and carefully weighed each word and each effect.*
*The impatient reader may do his own skipping, but for the*
*affectionate and leisurely, Stifter is here in full measure.*

THE Church observes various festivals that are ever dear to the heart. What more gracious than Whitsuntide: more sacred or of deeper significance than Easter. The portentous sadness of Holy Week and exaltation of the Sunday following, accompany us throughout life. One of the most beautiful of Church festivals comes in midwinter when nights are long and days are short, when the sun slants toward earth obliquely and snow mantles the fields: Christmas. In many countries the evening that precedes our Lord's nativity is known as Christmas Eve; in our region we call it Holy Eve, the day following Holy Day, and the night between, Holy Night. The Catholic Church observes Christmas, birthday of our Saviour, by magnificent and holiest ceremonial. In most places, midnight as the very hour of his birth is solemnized by ritual of great splendor, to which the bells ring out their heartsome invitation through the still darkness of the wintry air; then with their lanterns, along dim familiar paths, from snow-clad mountains, past forest-boughs encrusted with rime, through crackling orchards, folk flock to the church from which solemn strains are pouring,—the church rising from the heart of the village, enshrouded in ice-laden trees, its stately windows aglow.

Associated with the religious festival is a domestic one. In Christian lands far and wide it is the custom to portray for children the advent of the Christ-child—a child himself, most wondrous that ever dwelt on earth—as something joyous, resplendent, exalted, an ever-present influence throughout life that sometimes in old age, for one lost in sad or tender memories, revives bygone days as it passes on wings of fair colors, through the cheerless expanse of desolate night.

It is the custom to present children with gifts the Blessed Christ-child has brought; given usually on Christmas Eve when dusk has deepened into night. Candles are lit, generally a great many, that flicker together with the little waxlights on the fresh green branches of a small fir or spruce tree that has been set in the middle of the room.

The children must wait till the sign is given that the Blessed Christ-child has come and left his gifts. Only then is the door thrown wide for them to enter, and the sparkling radiance of the candles reveals objects hanging from the tree or spread out on the table, things beyond anything the children have imagined, things they dare

not touch but which, after they have received them as
gifts, they will carry about in their little arms and afterwards take with them to bed. If later in their dreams

they hear the midnight bells calling the grown-ups to
church, it will perhaps seem to them that the angelic
host is winging its way across high heaven, or that the
Christ-child is returning home after visiting children
everywhere and bringing to each, a wondrous gift.

Next day, when Christmas comes, how festive it is
early in the morning to be there in the warm room
dressed in their prettiest clothes, and later when Father

and Mother put on their Sunday best to go to church; or when at noon comes Christmas dinner—finer than any other in the whole year; and in the afternoon or toward evening, when friends call and, sitting about on chairs or benches, visit together as they look out at the wintry scene of falling snow or at the gray mist wreathing the mountains, or at the blood-red sun going down. Here and there about the room on stool or bench or window-sill, lie the magical gifts of the evening before—now familiar and all their own.

After this, the long winter departs; spring comes, then lingering summer—and when the mother again tells the story of the Christ-child, saying that his birthday is now to be celebrated and that he will visit the earth again, it seems to the children that his last coming has been inconceivably long ago, and as though the joys of that distant time lie veiled in remoteness.

Because this festival has such enduring power over us, with an afterglow reaching even into old age, we love to be with children when they joyously celebrate Christmas.

Among the high mountains of our country there is a little village with a small but needle-fine church-spire. Conspicuous above the green of abundant fruit-trees, this spire—because the slates are painted vermilion—can be seen far and wide against the faint blue of the mountains. The hamlet nestles in the very center of a fairly

wide valley that is an almost perfect ellipse. Besides the
church, a school-house, and a parish-house, there are a
few stately homes around a square with four linden-
trees and a stone cross in the center. These are not sim-
ple farmhouses, but a haven of handicrafts indispensable
to humanity, providing the mountain people with essential commodities. In the valley and scattered along
the mountain-sides are many little huts of a sort common to such regions—whose inhabitants belong to the
village, use its church and school, and support its craftsmen by buying their wares. Even more distant huts are
also part of the village, but, hidden away in the mountains, cannot be seen from the valley; the people rarely
come down among their fellow-parishioners. Often, indeed, they are obliged to keep their dead with them over
the winter till they can bring them to the valley for burial
after the snow has melted. The great man of the village
is the priest. The villagers regard him with veneration
and he, after a protracted stay in the valley, usually becomes used to isolation, stays on not unwillingly, and
then just goes on living there. At least since time im-
memorial no priest in the village has ever craved a
change, none has been unworthy of his calling.

There are no highways in the valley, merely cart-roads
with double wheel-tracks, along which the crops are
brought home on one-horse carts. Accordingly, few
strangers come to the valley; among these an occasional

wanderer, a nature-lover who lives for a time in the prettily-painted upper room of the inn, enjoying the mountain-view; or possibly an artist who sketches in his portfolio the delicate church-spire and beautiful rocky peaks.

The village people thus constitute a separate world, they know one another by name and are familiar with all the grandfathers' and great-grandfathers' tales. All mourn when anyone dies; all know the name of the new-born; they speak a language which is different from that used in the plain; they have their quarrels and settle them; they help one another, and if anything unusual happens, come flocking together.

They are steadfast, ever adhering to the ancient ways. If a stone is dislodged from a wall, that very stone is put back; the new houses are built like the old ones; damaged roofs are mended with shingles just like those they replace. If the cows on a farm are brindled, the calves on that farm must always be brindled; the color never changes.

South of the village you see a snowy mountain with dazzling horn-shaped peaks, rising, as it seems, from the house-tops themselves, but actually quite far away. All year round, summer and winter, there it is with its jutting crags and white expanses, looking down upon the valley. As the most prominent feature of the landscape and ever before the eyes of the villagers, the mountain has been the inspiration of many a tale. There is not a man, young or old, in the village who has not something to tell about its peaks and crags, its caves and crevasses, its streams and torrents—either something that has happened to himself or that he has heard about from others. This mountain is the pride of the village, as though the people had made it themselves, and with due respect to their honesty we can't swear to it that once in a while they would not fib for the honor and glory of their mountain. Besides being notable in itself, the mountain is actually profitable, since on the arrival of a party of mountain-climbers to make the ascent from the valley, the villagers serve as guides; and to have been a guide—had this or that experience, known this or that spot—is a distinction which affords anyone great satisfaction. When they sit together in the common room at the inn, they are always talking about their feats and strange adventures, never failing to mention what this or that traveler said and how much he had given them for their labors. The mountain also sends down from its snowy flanks streams that feed a lake in the forest, from which a brook emerges and flows merrily through the valley, driving the saw-mill, the grist-mill, and small machinery of various kinds, providing cleanliness for the village and watering the cattle. The forest tracts afford timber and also break the force of the avalanches. Through subterranean channels and loose soil at these altitudes water filters and, coursing veinlike through the valley, comes to the surface in little fountains and springs from which the people drink. And as time and again they offer strangers this unrivalled, much extolled water, they never stop to think how useful it is, accepting it simply as something that has always been there.

With regard to the change of seasons on the mountain, in winter the two pinnacles called 'horns' are snow-white and on clear days stand out in the dusky atmosphere with blinding brilliance; all the alpine meadows at the base of the summits are white then, as well as their sloping shoulders; even the precipitous rock-faces or walls as the people call them, are coated with a white velvet nap of hoar-frost and glazed with ice-tissue, so the entire mass towers like an enchanted castle above the darkish weight of gray forest mantling the base. In summer as the sun and temperate winds melt the snow on the steep gradients, the horns soar up, as the mountain people say, black into the sky, their surface marked only by exquisite little flecks and snow-veins. These veins, however, are not really white but the delicate milky blue of the distant snow on the darker blue rocks. At higher levels in hot weather, the alpine meadows about the horns never lose their blanket of eternal snow and it shines down on the verdure in the valley; but on the lower levels the recent winter snowfall—a mere down— melts away, and iridescent blue-green tints appear in the glacier that, now bared, greets the people in the valley.

Ascent from the mountain is made from the valley. One follows in the southerly direction a smooth, well-made road that leads by a neck or 'col' into another valley. A col is a mountain-range of moderate height, connecting two larger, more considerable, ranges; and following it, one passes between the ranges from one valley into another. The col which links the snow-mountain with the corresponding range opposite, is thickly studded with pines. At about the highest point of the road before it descends into the further valley, stands a little rustic memorial. One time a baker, carrying his basket over the col, was found dead at this spot. A picture of him and his basket with the pines about him, was painted on a tablet, fastened to scarlet post, and erected to mark the scene of the tragedy. At this marker, one turns off the road and follows along the col instead of making one's way straight down into the valley beyond. There is here an opening in the pines as if a road led into them and indeed during part of the year there is a path leading to the rustic memorial, by which timber is brought down and which afterwards disappears, overgrown by grass. Proceeding along this path which climbs gently, one comes at length to a clearing quite bare of trees, a barren heath with not so much as a bush, only scant heather, drought-inured mosses and small hardy plant-life. The ground then rises sharply and the ascent is long; one climbs in a worn groove or trench, which has the advantage of preventing one from losing the way over the

vast sameness of heath. After a time, rocky towers as of
a church thrust upward from the grassy floor and be-

18

tween these walls one keeps on climbing. Then more bare ridges appear, with scant vegetation, and one is breathing the air of the higher altitudes that lead direct to the ice-cap. At either side of the path is a steep wall, and it is this defile which joins the snow-mountain with the col. To scale the ice one skirts the margin for some time above the rocks that surround it, until one comes to the packed snow bridging the crevasses, snow hard enough at most seasons to bear the traveler's weight.

At the highest point of the icefield, the two horns rise from the snow. These peaks are difficult to ascend, moated as they are by snow, now wide, now narrow, and the *bergschrund* or rim must be compassed by a leap. Since the sheer verticals offer only scant ledges for foot-hold, most climbers are satisfied with reaching the *bergschrund* and from there enjoy as much of the pano-rama as is not cut off by the horn. Those wishing to reach the summit can do so only with the aid of spiked shoes, ropes, and cleats.

There are other mountains besides this one on the southern horizon, but none so high. In the early autumn they too are covered with snow, and on into late spring. Summer, however, eats the snow away and the rocks gleam in the sun with a gentle allure, and the rich green of the lower forest is intersected by broad-lying violet shadows—a scene so lovely, one could look at it all one's life and never tire of it.

19

Along the valley in other directions—to the north, the east and the west—the mountains stretch away into the distance, on and on, but lower, with occasional pastures and patches of tilled ground on the slopes and higher up forest clearings and alpine huts, the skyline marked by a delicate sawtooth edge that is an indication of the moderate height of the range; whereas on the southern horizon the mountains, although clothed with magnificent forest, sweep along with smooth outline against the luminous sky.

Standing in about the middle of the valley, one has the impression that not a single road leads either into or out of the basin—an illusion familiar to anyone who has spent much time in the mountains—while in reality there are several roads leading not only into the northern plains, but also toward the south, where the valley appears to be closed in by walls of perpendicular rock, there is the col path.

The little village is called Gschaid, and the snow-mountain that looks down upon its houses is called Gars.

On the other side of the col, with the beaten path from the wayside shrine leading down to it, is a much more beautiful and fertile valley than that of Gschaid. As one comes into it, one encounters the stately market-town of Millsdorf. It is a sizeable town with several kinds of mills and a number of buildings in which trades and crafts are housed. The inhabitants are more prosperous

than those of Gschaid, and although the valleys are only
three hours' distance apart—a trifling matter to mountain
people, used as they are to great distances and inured
to hardship—manners and customs in the two valleys
are so different and they are so unlike in appearance,
one would think that untold miles separated them. This
is often the case in mountainous regions not only because
of their varying positions—more or less propitious—
with relation to the sun, but also as a result of character,
which has led the inhabitants to choose differing occupa-
tions. But in one respect they are all alike, they cling
to what is traditional and to the ancient ways of their
forefathers, never seem to miss the bustle of traffic,
love their own valley ardently, and could scarcely exist
away from it.

Months, sometimes a year, may pass before anyone
from Gschaid crosses into the valley beyond to visit the
great market-town, Millsdorf. And although the same is
true of the people of Millsdorf, yet being in communica-
tion with other parts of the country around them, they
are not as sequestered as the people of Gschaid. There
is even a road which might be called a highway, the
length of their valley, and many a traveler, many a wanderer, goes on his way without a suspicion that north of
him on the farther side of the lordly snow-mountain,
lies a valley with a goodly scattering of houses, and a
hamlet with tapering church-spire.

One of the trades supplying the people in this valley with essential commodities is the shoemaker's—indispensable the world over where human beings are no longer in the primitive stage. These valley people of Gschaid, be it said, are so far beyond it that they need the very stoutest and most durable highland footwear. The shoemaker—with a minor exception—is the only one in the valley. His house in Gschaid fronts on the square—among the better houses—and with its gray walls, white window-sills and green shutters, looks out on the four linden-trees. It has, on the ground-floor, the work-room, the journeymen's room, a large and a small living-room, the little shop, together with kitchen, larder, and such cupboards as pertain to them. On the second floor, that is in the gable-end, is an upper chamber, a formal best room in which stand two imposing beds, well-polished and well-stocked wardrobes, also a china closet with dishes, an inlaid table, upholstered chairs, a little recessed wall safe or cupboard for savings, pictures of saints, two exquisite time-pieces, and shooting-match prizes. Lastly, in a special cabinet of their own, with glass front, hang rifles for target practice and for hunting, with everything pertaining to them.

Adjoining the shoemaker's house is a much smaller one separated only by an arched passage, built in the same style, and a component part of the other—a detail of the whole. It consists of one room with the usual ad-

juncts. It is for the use of the owner when he has transferred the property to his son or successor—a retirement-annex as it is called—in which he and his wife may spend their last years. Then again, the small house will be vacant, awaiting a new occupant.

The shoemaker's house has a stable and barn at the rear, since everyone who lives in the valley—tradesman or not—tills the ground, obtaining thus his nourishing food. Behind the buildings, as with any of the better houses in Gschaid, is a garden which furnishes vegetables, fruit, and, for festive occasions, flowers. As in most mountain regions, bee-keeping is customary, with straw hives in the garden.

The aforementioned minor exception, the only rival of the shoemaker, was Old Tobias who, in reality, was no rival at all, since by that time he merely did cobbling. He had plenty of work and it never occurred to him to compete with the fashionable shoemaker on the square, especially as the latter often provided him with patches, pieces of sole and the like, without charging for them. In the summertime Old Tobias would sit under the elder-bushes at the end of the village, working away. All about him were low shoes and mountain shoes, but it was the same with each pair—they were old, scuffed, discolored, and muddy. There were no high-legged boots among them because these were not worn in the village and valley of Gschaid. The only two persons who had such boots, the priest and the school-master, had their mending as well as their new work done by the shoemaker on the square. In winter Old Tobias stayed in his cottage

behind the elder-bushes, which, since wood in Gschaid is not expensive, was always nice and warm.

The shoemaker on the square, before he inherited his house, had been a chamois-poacher and in general, so people said, not too model a youth. In school he had always been one of the best pupils. Later he had learned his father's trade, and after working as a wandering journeyman, had finally come back to the village. But instead of wearing a black hat as becomes a tradesman—such as his father had worn all his life—he perched a green one on his head, stuck every available feather in it, and strutted about wearing the shortest frieze coat in the valley, whereas his father had always worn a dark coat, preferably black—since he was a man of trade—and invariably cut long. The young shoemaker was to be seen on every dance floor and at every bowling alley. If anyone tried to reason with him, he just whistled a tune. He and his marksman's rifle were at every shooting match in the neighborhood and sometimes he carried home a prize—treasured by him as a great trophy. The prize was usually a set of coins artistically arranged. But the shoemaker, in order to win it, had to disburse many more similar coins, in his usual spendthrift fashion. He went to all the hunts in the neighborhood and had quite a reputation for being a good marksman. Sometimes, however, he fared forth alone with his blunderbuss and spiked shoes, and it was rumored that he had once received a serious wound on his head.

In Millsdorf just where the town begins, as you come in by the road from Gschaid, there lived a dyer with a thriving business in which he employed many workmen; and—something unheard of in the valley—he even made use of machinery. He was, moreover, the possessor of extensive farmlands. To woo the daughter of this prosperous dyer, the shoemaker would trudge all the way over the mountains. Noted far and wide for her beauty, she was also admired for her virtue, decorum, and housewifely accomplishments. Nevertheless, it would seem, the shoemaker attracted her attention. The dyer would not allow him to enter the house; and whereas the beautiful daughter had not previously gone to public places or taken part in festivities and had rarely been seen away from home, now she went nowhere but to church or into the garden or from one room to another in the house.

Some time after the death of his parents when he had become proprietor of the house where he now lived all alone, the shoemaker changed into a wholly different person. Whereas till then he was always rollicking about, he now sat in his shop, hammering away on sole-leather, day and night. He boasted that no one could make better shoes and footgear, and engaged only the best workmen whom he nagged and pestered a good deal as they sat at their work, making them follow his instructions and do exactly as he told them. The result was that not only did everyone in Gschaid who had always before got footwear from neighboring valleys, now come to him, but the entire valley as well. And as time went on, even people from Millsdorf and other valleys came to have their footwear made by the shoemaker of Gschaid. His fame traveled even into the plain so that many people who intended to climb the mountains had their special shoes made by him.

He kept his house spick and span, and shoes, mountain-shoes, and high boots gleamed on the shelves of the store room; and on Sundays when folk from all over the valley flocked to the village and stood around on the square with its four linden-trees, they liked to go over to the shoemaker's and peep through the windows at all the people buying and ordering shoes.

In keeping with his love for the mountains, mountain shoes were his best work, and he used to say in the common room at the inn that no one could show him a mountain shoe made by anyone else that could compare with one of his. "They haven't the knack," he would add. "They can work all their lives and still they don't know how a shoe like that should be made, so the nail-starred design has the heads of the nails at exactly the right place on the sole, with just the right amount of iron in them; so that the shoe is hard on the outside and no loose stone, however sharp, can be felt, and the inside lies as soft and tender against the foot as a glove."

The shoemaker had had a big book made in which he entered all finished work, the names of those who had furnished the material, and of those who had bought the finished product,—together with a word about the quality of the goods, and this book was kept in the large chest in the store.

29

Now, although the dyer's beautiful daughter stayed
at home most of the time and visited neither relatives
nor friends, the shoemaker from Gschaid managed it
so that she should catch a glimpse of him when she went
to church, walked about the garden, or looked from the
windows of her room. Because of this constant gazing,
the dyer's wife by long, insistent, unremitting supplica-
tions induced her stiff-necked husband to give in, and
the shoemaker (who had, after all, mended his ways)
carried off the beautiful and wealthy maiden of Millsdorf as his bride. The dyer, however, was a headstrong
person. The right sort of man, he said, has an occupa-
tion, makes it thrive and grow, and thereby supports his
wife, children, himself and domestics; he keeps his house
in order and lays by a goodly nest-egg which is the only
thing that gives a man dignity and standing in the world.
Thus it was that the only dowry his daughter received
was a well-filled hope chest, the rest was the husband's
concern—for the present and in future. The dyeworks in
Millsdorf with its farmland was a business worthwhile
in itself, besides reflecting credit on its owner; and since
all of it was, in a sense, capital, he would give none of
it away. But once he and his wife had died, the dyeworks
and farmland would fall to their only daughter, namely
the shoemaker's wife in Gschaid; and the shoemaker and
his wife might then do with them as they pleased: provided, that is, that the heirs were worthy; should they

be unworthy, they would get only the legal share, the inheritance going to their children, and if there were none, to other relatives. Nor did the shoemaker make any demands, showing proudly that all he had wanted was to win the dyer's beautiful daughter, and that he was well able to keep her and care for her as she had been kept and cared for at home. And, as his wife, he dressed her not only better than any of the women of Gschaid and of the valley were dressed, but better even than she had been at home, and meat and drink and everything about the house had to be better and choicer than anything she had enjoyed in her father's house. And to spite his father-in-law, he bought more and more land, so that he came finally to possess a considerable property.

Since the people of Gschaid seldom leave their valley and almost never go to Millsdorf, from which they are separated by mountain and by customs—and since, furthermore, no one ever leaves his valley to settle in a neighboring one—although removals to great distances occur—and lastly since no girl ever leaves her valley except on the rare occasion when, obeying the dictates of love, as a bride, she follows her husband into another valley—so it came about that after the beautiful daughter of the dyer of Millsdorf married the shoemaker of Gschaid she was still regarded by the people of Gschaid as a stranger; and although they were not unkind to her, and even loved her for her charm and virtue, there was always something, reserve or a sort of shy respect, that kept her from enjoying the same familiarity and warm intimacy that existed between the people that belonged to the valley. That's the way it was and no use talking about it. And the finer clothes and easier domestic life of the shoemaker's wife only made it worse.

After having been married a year she bore her husband a son, and several years later, a daughter. She felt, however, that he did not love the children as much as she thought he ought to, and as she herself loved them; for he looked so serious most of the time and was always preoccupied with his work. He rarely petted or played with them, and always addressed them quietly as one speaks to grown persons. In the matter of food, clothes and all material things, however, his care for them was above reproach.

At first, the dyer's wife often came to Gschaid and the young couple also at times went over to Millsdorf to attend church fairs and on other festive occasions. But after the children were born, things were different. Mothers may love their children and tenderly long for them when they are absent, but a grandmother's longing for her grandchildren amounts almost to a morbid craving. The dyer's wife would often come over to Gschaid to see the children, bring them presents, stay a while, and then, after giving them some good advice, depart. But

34

when age and health made these frequent journeys in-
advisable and the dyer for that reason objected to them,
a different plan was devised, everything was reversed,
and the children visited their grandmother instead. Their

mother herself would often take them in the carriage
or they would be entrusted to a maidservant, and driven
in a buggy over the col, well bundled up since they were
still of tender years. But when older, they would go on
foot, accompanied by their mother or a maid, and when
the lad had grown strong, knowing, and self-reliant, they

let him take the familiar road over the col by himself, and even, when he begged to take his little sister along, if the weather was good would allow her to go with him. There was nothing unusual about this in Gschaid, since the people were hardy walkers, and parents—especially a man like the shoemaker, admired physical strength and were glad to see it in their children.

So it came about that the two children went over the col oftener than any of the other villagers and in this way, like their mother who had always been treated as a stranger in Gschaid, the children became strangers too; and were hardly Gschaid children, but belonged half to Millsdorf.

Conrad, the boy, already gave evidence of his father's serious disposition, and Susanna the little girl, named for her mother and called Sanna for short, had unbounded faith in his knowledge, judgment and physical strength, and followed unquestioningly wherever he led, just as their mother accepted their father's guidance and never questioned his superior judgment in all matters.

On clear days the children could be seen early in the morning, making their way down the valley, crossing the meadow and coming to the place where the col forest looks down upon it. Going up toward the forest they would keep to the path, finally reaching the highest point, and before noon be descending the open meadows on the other side, toward Millsdorf. Conrad then showed

Sanna the ones belonging to their grandfather; as they walked across the fields he told her about the various kinds of grain; they would look at the cloth-lengths hanging from poles under the rafters to dry, and capering in the wind or blown into antic postures; then they would hear the fulling-mill and the pounding in the tannery built by their grandfather beside the brook, for fullers and tanners; and now, turning a corner of the field, they were soon entering the garden through the back gate where they were welcomed by their grandmother. She always seemed to know when they were coming, would watch from the window, and seeing Sanna's red kerchief shining in the sun would recognize them from far away.

She then led them through wash-house and press into the living-room, made them sit down, and would not let them open their neckerchiefs or spencers lest they catch cold. After the midday meal they were allowed to go out and play, run about the house, or do anything they liked, provided it was not indecorous or forbidden. The dyer, always at table with them, asked them about their school work, dwelling particularly on the subjects they should study. In the afternoon, even before it was time, their grandmother would begin urging them to start back, so that they would not be late reaching home. Although the dyer had given his daughter no dowry and vowed that until his death none of his fortune should

37

be given away, his wife had no such scruples, and not only gave the children all kinds of things when they visited her, frequently even pieces of money of considerable value, but also and invariably made up two little bundles in which she put such things as she thought they might need or that would give them pleasure. And even if they had the same things in the shoemaker's house in Gschaid—as good as one could desire—their grandmother would give for the sheer pleasure of giving, and they would carry her gifts home with them as something very precious. So it always happened that the day before Christmas they would take home carefully wrapped well-sealed packages, quite unaware that they were presents they would receive that same evening.

Their grandmother's bundling them off always long before it was time merely resulted in the children's loitering at this spot or that along the way. They liked to sit by the hazel-trees on the col and crack nuts with stones; or if there were no nuts, play with leaves or little sticks or with the pine-cones that drop from the pine and fir branches in early spring. Sometimes Conrad would tell little stories to his sister, or coming to the wayside shrine, would take her a little way up the side-road at the left toward the heights, saying that that was the way to Snow-mountain, that there were crags and huge boulders up there, chamois scampering, and great birds flying about. He often took her even high up above the tree-line, and they would gaze at the dry grass and stunted heather; but he led her back again in time and they would have returned before the gloaming.

One winter, the day before Christmas, when in the valley of Gschaid early dawn had broadened into day, a faint clear-weather haze overspread the sky, so that the sun creeping up in the south-east could be seen only as an indistinct reddish ball; furthermore, the air was mild, almost warm in the valley and even in the upper reaches of the sky as indicated by the unchanging forms of the motionless clouds. So the shoemaker's wife said to the children: "Since it is such a fine day and since it has not rained for a long time and the roads are hard, and since yesterday your father gave you permission, provided it was the right kind of day, you may go over to Millsdorf to see your grandmother; but first you must ask your father again."

The children, still in their night-clothes, ran into the adjoining room where their father was talking with a customer, and begged him—since it was such a beautiful day—to give them his permission again. And as soon as they had his consent, they ran back to their mother who then dressed them both with great care, or rather, dressed the little girl, for the lad was able to dress by himself and was ready long before his mother had finished bundling up the little one in warm clothes. Then, when everything was right, she said: "Now Conrad, lis-

39

ten carefully. Since I am letting your sister go with you, you must start for home in plenty of time and you must not loiter on the way. As soon as dinner at your grandmother's is over, you must leave at once and come straight home. The days are short now, and the sun sets early."

"Yes, Mother, I know," said Conrad.

"And watch out for Sanna, so she doesn't fall or get herself overheated."

"Yes, Mother."

"Well, God protect you. Now go tell your father you are leaving."

The lad slung a calfskin pouch over his shoulder by a strap—a perquisite deftly sewn by his father—and the children went into the next room to bid him farewell. They were soon back, and after their mother had made the sign of the cross over them in blessing, they skipped merrily off down the street.

They walked quickly along the square and the row of houses, past the picket fences of the orchards, and finally came into the open. The sun had already risen over the woodlands on the eastern heights that were still shot with wefts of pale mist,—the dull reddish ball keeping pace with them through the leafless branches of the crab-apple trees.

There was no snow anywhere in the valley; the higher mountains which had been glistening for weeks, were covered with it; the lower ones stood snowless and silent in their pine-mantle of green and fallow brown of bare branches. The ground was not yet frozen and would have been quite dry because of the long stretch without rain, if the cold had not overlaid it with a faint moisture, which instead of making it slippery, had made it all the safer and so resilient that walking was easy. The sparse grass still on the meadows and particularly along the ditches, had an autumn look. There was no frost on the grass and if one looked closely, not even any dew, all of which interpreted locally was a sign of imminent rain.

Down toward the far edge of the meadow was a mountain brook crossed by a high plank. The children walked along the plank and looked down. There was scarcely any water in the brook, a mere thread of intense blue on the stony bed, the dry pebbles having become perfectly white in the long weeks without rain, and the scantness as well as the color of the water meant bitter cold at the higher altitudes—cold that held the ground in a vise so it could not make the brook turbid with sediment, and hardening the ice so the core gave off only a few clear drops.

From the foot-bridge the children raced over the meadows, closer and closer to the woodland.

They came at last to the outskirts of the forest and went on into it.

When they had climbed into the higher woods of the neck, the long ruts in the cart-road were not soft as they had been in the valley, but firm, because they were frozen;

in some places hard enough to bear the children's weight. Child-like, they no longer kept to the smooth path by the road but walked in the ruts, seeing which ridges would bear their weight. When in an hour they had reached the

crest of the col, the ground was by that time so hard their steps rang and the clods were like iron.

Sanna was the first to notice at the shrine erected in memory of the baker, that the red post supporting the tablet was no longer there. They went closer and saw that it lay in the dry grass that stood up like pale straw,

partly concealing it. They did not see why the post should
be lying there—whether it had been thrown down or had
fallen of itself—but they did see the wood rotted where it
came out of the ground, and that it might have toppled
over of itself; but as it lay there, they were glad to be
able to have a closer look at the picture and the inscrip-
tion. When they had studied it all,—the basket with the
rolls, the whitish hands of the baker, his closed eyes, his
gray coat, and the pines about him—had spelled out the
legend and then said it out loud—they proceeded on
their way.

Another hour and the dark woods on both sides were
dim behind them; thin-set trees, part single oaks, part
birch and clusters of scrub, met the eye, continuing with
them a distance and shortly after, the children were run-
ning down through the meadows into the valley of Millsdorf.

Although this valley is considerably lower than that of
Gschaid and is therefore so much warmer that harvest
begins two weeks earlier than in Gschaid, the ground
here was frozen too; and when the children came to their
grandfather's tannery and fulling-mill, they found in the
road where the wheels scatter drops of water, thin sheets
of cat's-ice, ever a delight to children.

Their grandmother had seen them and coming out to
meet them, took Sanna's little icy hands in hers and led
the children inside.

43

She undid their wraps, had fresh wood put in the stove, and asked what had happened on the way over.

When they had answered, she said: "That's good, that's all right, I am glad you came, but this time you must be off very soon, the days are short and it is getting colder; nothing was frozen in Millsdorf this morning."

"Nor in Gschaid," said the lad.

"See? You must hurry then so you won't be too cold by evening," answered their grandmother.

Then she asked how their mother was, how was their father, and had anything happened in Gschaid.

After these inquiries she busied herself with the meal, made sure it would be on the table earlier than usual, and herself prepared little appetizing things for the children that she knew they liked. Then the dyer was called in, the children sat down at the table laid for them as for grown-ups, ate with their grandfather and grandmother, the latter piling good things on their plates. After dinner, she patted Sanna's cheek, quite rosy by this time. Then she hustled about here and there, packing to overflowing the lad's calfskin pouch, besides stuffing things into his pockets. She also put divers things into Sanna's little pockets, gave them each a piece of bread to eat on the way, and in the bag, she told them, were two rolls in case they became very hungry.

"For your mother," she said, "I am giving you some well-roasted coffee-beans, and in the very tightly wrapped

44

bottle with the stopper is some black coffee extract better than your mother herself usually makes; she can taste some just as it is; it is a veritable tonic, so strong the merest sip warms the stomach so that you cannot feel chilled even on the coldest of winter days. The other things in the bag, in the cardboard box wrapped with paper, you are to take home without opening."

After a word or two more with the children, she said they must go.

"Take good care, Sanna," she said, "not to get chilled; don't get overheated; and don't you run up over the meadows and under the trees. The wind may come up toward evening and then you will have to go slower. Greetings to Father and Mother, and tell them we wish them a right merry Christmas." She kissed them each on the cheek, and hastened them forth. But she accompanied them through the garden, let them out by the rear gate, shut it again, and came back into the house.

The children went past the thin sheets of cat's-ice beside their grandfather's mill, crossed the fields and turned up toward the rising meadows.

When they had come to the heights covered with scattered trees and thickets of scrub, already mentioned, some few snowflakes floated slowly down.

"See there, Sanna," said the lad. "I knew it would snow; remember when we left home, we could still see the sun, as red as the lamp over the Holy Sepulcher in

45

church during Holy Week, and now we can't see even the faintest ray and there's only gray fog up there over the tree-tops. That always means snow."

The children walked on more briskly, and Sanna was delighted whenever she caught a falling flake on the sleeve of her dark coat and it did not melt for a long time. When finally they came to the further fringe of the Mills-dorf heights before entering the dark woods on the col, the serried wall of pines was already prettily flecked with the fast-falling snow. They now entered the deep woods, the longest part of the remaining way home. Up and up, from the fringe of the forest, the ground rises till one comes to the red post of the wayside shrine, from where as we said before the road turns off down to Gschaid. The ascent through the woods is so steep from the Mills-dorf side that the road does not lead straight up but in wide serpentines, west to east and east to west. At each side of the road, the whole way up to the shrine and down to the meadows of Gschaid, there are impenetrable densely towering woods that thin only a little as one gains the valley level and comes out on the meadows in the valley of Gschaid. The col itself, though but a small link between two great ranges, would, if set on the floor of the valley, be a considerable mountain-chain.

The first thing that struck the children on entering the woods, was that the frozen ground had a whitish look as though meal had been scattered; the heads of some of the

grasses by the road and amongst the trees were drooping
with the weight of snow on them and the many green

pine and fir ends, reaching out like hands, held up little
thistledown pyramids.

"Is it snowing at home now, where father is?" asked
Sanna.

"Certainly," answered her brother, "getting colder,
too, and you'll see tomorrow, the whole pond will be
frozen over."

"Yes, Conrad," said the child.

47

She all but doubled her short steps to keep pace with the lad as he strode along.

They went steadily up the winding road, now west to east, now east to west. The wind predicted by their grandmother had not come up; the air, on the contrary, was so still not a twig or a branch stirred; in fact it felt warmer in the woods, as is usual, in winter, among spaced objects like tree-trunks, and the flakes kept falling thicker and thicker so the ground was already white, and the woods began to gray and take on a dusty look, with snow settling upon the garments and hats of both the boy and his sister.

The children were delighted. They set their feet on the soft down and eagerly looked for places where it seemed thicker so they could make believe they were already deep in it. They did not shake the snow from their clothing. There had descended upon everything a pervading sense of peace. Not the sound of a bird, although a few birds usually flit about the woods even in winter, and the children on the way to Millsdorf that morning had heard them twitter; they did not see any, either flying or on branches, and the whole forest was as though dead.

Since the footprints behind were their own and the snow ahead lay white and unbroken, it was evident that they were the only ones crossing the col that day.

They kept on in the same direction, now coming toward trees, now leaving them behind, and where the

underbrush was thick they could even see the snow lying
on the twigs.

Their spirits were still rising, for the flakes fell thicker
and thicker and in a little while they did not have to look
for snow to wade in, because it lay so thick it felt soft to
the feet everywhere, and even came up around their
shoes; and it was so still, so intimate, it seemed as if they
could almost hear the rustle of the flakes settling on the
pine needles.

"Shall we see the baker's post today, I wonder," asked
the little girl, "for it's fallen down and will be snowed
on, so the red will be white."

"We'll see it, just the same," said the lad, "we'll see
it lying there even if the snow does fall on it and make
it white for it's a good thick post and the black iron cross
on top would always stick up."

"Yes, Conrad."

In the meantime, while they kept on, the snow became
so thick they could see only the nearest trees.

They could not feel the hardness of the road or the
ridges of the wheel-ruts; the road was an even softness
everywhere because of the snow, and one could distin-
guish it only as it wound on through the forest smooth
and white like a ribbon. Every bough was mantled in
fairest white.

The children were walking now in the middle of the
road, their little feet ploughing through snow that slowed

their steps, for the going was harder. The lad pulled his jacket together at the collar so the snow would not fall on the back of his neck, and shoved his hat further down about his ears for protection. He also drew the shawl tighter, that his mother had folded about his little sister, and pulled it out over her forehead in a little roof.

The wind predicted by their grandmother had not yet come up, but on the other hand the snowfall had by degrees become so heavy that after a while even the nearest trees were indistinct and stood in the blur like powdery sacks.

The children pushed on. They shrank down into their coats and pushed on.

Sanna took hold of the shoulder-strap by which Conrad's bag was suspended, and with her little hand clutching the strap, they wended their way.

They were still not as far as the wayside memorial. The lad could not be sure of the time because there was no sun, and everything was the same monotonous gray.

"Will we be at the post soon?" asked Sanna.

"I don't know," answered her brother. "This time, I can't make out the trees, or the road because it is so white. We may not see the post at all, because there is so much snow it will be covered up, and hardly a grass-blade or arm of the cross will stick out. But that's nothing. We'll just keep straight on; the road leads through the trees and when it gets to the place where the post is, then it

50

will start downhill and we keep right on it and when it comes out of the woods we are in Gschaid meadows; then comes the foot-bridge, and we're not far from home."

On they went, climbing the path. Their footprints did

not show for long now, since the unusually heavy snow blotted them out at once. The quick-falling flakes no longer made even a ticking sound on the needles as they fell but imperceptibly merged with the deep white already mantling the ground.

The children drew their wraps still closer to keep the ever-falling snow from working in on all sides.

They quickened their steps and the road was still climbing.

After a great while they had not yet reached the place where the memorial post was supposed to be, from which the path to Gschaid turned off down hill.

At last they came to a tract with not a tree on it.

"I don't see any trees," said Sanna.

"Perhaps the road is so wide we can't see them because of the snow," said the lad.

"Yes, Conrad," said the little one.

After a time the lad came to a halt and said, "I don't see any trees myself now. We must be out of the forest. Yet the road is still going up. Let's stop a minute and look about. Perhaps we can see something."

But they did not see anything. They stared up through wan nothingness into the sky. As during a hailstorm, when leaden striations slant downward from the massed white or greenish cloudbanks, so here; and the mute downfall continued.

The place was a circular patch of white ground, nothing else.

"You know, Sanna," said the lad, "we are on that dry grass I have often brought you to in summer, where we used to sit and look at the grassy floor sloping up, where the beautiful herb-tufts grow. We shall turn right now, and be going down hill."

"Yes, Conrad."

"The days are short, as Grandmother said and as you know yourself, so we must hurry."

"Yes, Conrad," said the little one.

"Wait a minute, I am going to snug you up a bit," said the lad.

He took off his hat, put it on Sanna and tied the two ribbons under her chin. The kerchief she had been wearing was too slight protection, whereas the profusion of curls on his head was so thick, snow would rest on them a long time before the wet and cold could penetrate. Then he took off his little fur jacket and drew it on his sister, up over her little arms. With only his shirt to protect him now, he tied about his shoulders the little shawl Sanna had been wearing. It would do for him, he thought, if they could just walk at a brisk pace.

He took his sister by the hand and thus they started on again.

With trustful eyes the little thing gazed up at the prevailing gray all about them and accompanied him willingly; only that her small hurrying feet could not keep up with him as he strove onward like someone bent on settling a thing once and for all.

They were going on now with the dogged endurance that children and animals have, not knowing what is ahead or when their reserves may give out.

However, as they went, they could not tell whether they were going down the mountain or not. They had soon turned downhill to the right but then came to elevations leading up. Often they encountered sheer rises they had to avoid; and a hollow in which they were walking led them around in a curve. They climbed hummocks that became steeper under their feet than they expected; and what they had deemed a descent was level ground or a depression, or went on as an even stretch.

"But where are we, Conrad?" asked the child.

"I don't know," he answered. "If only my eyes could make out something and I could get my bearings."

But on every side was nothing but a blinding whiteness, white everywhere that none the less drew its ever-narrowing circle about them, paling beyond into fog that came down in waves, devouring and shrouding everything till there was nothing but the voracious snow.

"Wait, Sanna," said the lad, "let's stand still a little and listen and see if we can't hear something,—a sound from down there in the valley perhaps, a dog or a bell or the mill, or maybe someone calling; we ought to be able to hear something, at any rate, then we'll know which way to go."

They stood still, but heard nothing. They stood a little longer, but there was nothing to be heard, not a single sound, not the faintest except their breath; indeed in the stillness reigning, it was as if they could hear the snow falling on their very eyelashes. Their grandmother's prediction had still not come true, the wind had not risen and, what was rare for those regions, not a breath stirred overhead, anywhere.

After waiting a considerable time, they went on again.

"Never mind, Sanna," said her brother, "don't be frightened, just follow me and I'll get you there yet. If it would only stop snowing."

She was not afraid but lifted her feet as well as she could and followed him. He led her on through the white fluctuating all-pervading pearly opaqueness.

After a time rocks suddenly loomed up dark and indistinct in the white luminescence—they had almost run into them—rocks that rose so sheer scarcely any snow could cling to them.

"Sanna, Sanna," he said, "there are the rocks, let's go on, let's go on."

They went on, had to, between rocks and along the base. The rocks admitted of swerving neither to right nor left, leading on in one narrow hollowed-out channel. After a time the children left them behind and could not see them any more. As unexpectedly as they had come in among them, as unexpectedly they came out. Again there was nothing about them but whiteness, with no dark obstructions looming up. It seemed just one vast volume of white and yet one could not see three feet ahead; everything was closed in, so to speak, by a mysterious white obscurity, and since there were no shadows it was impossible to judge the size of objects and the children did not know whether to step up or down until steepness raised the foot and compelled it to climb.

"My eyes hurt," said Sanna.

"Don't look at the snow," answered the lad, "but at the clouds. Mine have been hurting a good while, but it doesn't matter, I have to look at the snow anyhow, in order to watch the road. But don't be scared. I will get you down to Gschaid yet."

"Yes, Conrad."

They went on again; but however they went or however they turned it didn't seem ever as if they were beginning to go down hill. At either side steep rooflike formations led upward, and they walked between, but always up. Whenever they went outside the 'roofs' and turned downhill, it became so steep immediately they had to come back; their little feet often encountered jagged objects, and they were constantly avoiding hummocks.

They noticed also that whenever their feet sank deeper in the fresh snow, they did not feel an earthy firmness beneath but something different, like already frozen, older snow. But they kept on, walking fast and steadily. If they stopped, everything was silent, unbelievably silent; when they walked they heard the shuffling of their feet, nothing else; for the pall of flakes descended without a sound, such heavy snow one could fairly see it wax deep. The children themselves were so thickly covered they did not stand out against the general whiteness and

56

would not have been able to see each other if they had been more than a few steps apart.

It was a blessing the snow was dry as sand, so it shook off easily and slid from their feet and little mountain shoes and stockings without caking and soaking them.

At last they again came to something with form, immense shapes heaped in gigantic confusion, covered with snow that was sifting everywhere into the crevices; the children had, moreover, almost stumbled on them before they had seen them. They went close to look.

Ice—nothing but ice.

There were great slabs lying, covered with snow but on the edges glassy green ice showed; there were mounds of what looked like pushed up foam, the sides dull but with inward glimmers as if crystals and splinters of precious stones had been jumbled together; there were, besides, great rounded bosses engulfed in snow, slabs and other shapes, slanting or upright,—as high as the church steeple or houses in Gschaid. Some were eroded into cavities through which an arm, a head, a body, or a great cartload of hay could pass. All these irregular shapes had been driven into one another or upright, and stood out in the form of roofs or eaves; and overlying and overlapping them were great white cat's-paws of snow. Even a fearsome black boulder huge as a house lay tilted up under the ice, resting on its point, so that snow could not cling to the sides. And not this stone merely, but others, and yet larger ones, locked in the ice, which one did not notice at first, formed a wall of Cyclopean debris along the ice rim.

"There must have been a great deal of water here, because there is so much ice," said Sanna.

"No, it wasn't made by water," answered her brother, "it's the ice of the mountain, and always here since God made it so."

"Yes, Conrad," said Sanna.

"We are as far as the ice now," said the lad, "we are on the mountain, you know, Sanna, the one that looks so white in the sun from the garden. Now think hard about this. Do you remember when we were sitting in the garden, how pleasant it was, how the bees hummed round us, how sweet the lindens smelled, and how the sun was shining so bright on us?"

"Yes, Conrad, I remember."

"We would look at the mountain too. We saw how blue it was, blue as the gentle sky, we saw snow up there even though it was summer in the village and hot, and the wheat was getting ripe."

"Yes, Conrad."

"And down where the snow ends, you see all manner of colors if you look hard,—green, blue, and a whitish color—that is the ice that looks so small from down below because you are so far away, and that, as Father said, is going to be there as long as the world lasts. And

then I've often noticed that the blue color keeps on below the ice,—probably stones, I've thought, or maybe ploughed ground and pastures, and then come the pine woods that go down and down, and all kinds of rocks in between, then the green meadows, then the woods with leaves, and then our own meadows and fields in the valley of Gschaid. Now you see, Sanna, we are at the ice and from here we will go down over the blue color and through the woods where the rocks are, then over the meadows and then through the woods with the leaves, and then we shall be in the valley of Gschaid and then it will be easy to find our village."

"Yes, Conrad," said the little one.

The children went on into the ice wherever they could find a place to step.

They were just tiny moving dots among the formidable masses.

As they peered in beneath the projecting slabs, almost as if instinct were impelling them to seek shelter, they walked along in a broad deeply-scored channel that led straight out of the ice, like the bed of a stream, dried up now and covered with new-fallen snow. Where it emerged it was vaulted over with ice, beautifully arched like a canopy. Following the channel, they went in—deeper and deeper. It was entirely dry, and they had smooth ice to walk on. But the whole cavern was blue, bluer than anything on earth, a blue deeper and finer than the vault of heaven itself, blue as azure glass with a faint light inside. There were massive ribs overhead, and more delicate ones, with pendant icicles, point lace, and tassels, the way leading further still—they knew not how far— but they did not go on. It might even have been pleasant in the cave, it was warm, no snow was falling; but it was so fearsome a blue the children were frightened and ran out again. They walked on a while in the hollowed bed of the stream and then climbed up over the side.

They kept along the edge of the ice as far as they could thread through the detritus and creep between the great slabs.

"We have to get up over this and then we can run down, away from the ice," said Conrad.

"Yes," said Sanna, and clung tight to him.

They now struck a downward course through the snow, one that was to lead them into the valley. But they did not get far. Another river of ice, heaved up in a pile like a gigantic barricade, lay across the soft snow and seemed almost to be reaching out arms to the left and the right. Under the blanket of white that hid it there were green-ish, bluish, leaden, black, even yellow and reddish glim-mers from the sides.

They now had a better perspective since the unprece-dented unwearying snow was thinning and flakes were coming down only as on ordinary snowy days. With the fortitude of ignorance they clambered up on the ice to cross the protruding tongue of the glacier and then descend on the farther side. They crept through slits, planted their feet on any snow-capped projection whether rock or ice, helped with their hands, crawled where they could not walk, their light bodies working on up until they had scaled the inside of the barrier and were on top.

They had intended to climb down the other side.

There was no other side.

As far as the eye could reach there was only ice. Pointed masses and irregular clumps thrusting up from the fearsome snow-encrusted ice. Instead of a barricade that could be surmounted, with snow beyond, as they had expected, yet other walls of ice rose from the buttress, cracked and fissured, with innumerable meandering blue veins, and beyond these walls, others like them; and beyond, others, until the falling snow blurred the distance in its veil of gray.

"Sanna, we cannot go over there," said the lad.

"No," said the little one.

"We shall just turn around and get down somewhere else."

"Yes, Conrad."

The children then tried to climb down at the place where they had clambered up, but were not able. There was nothing but ice, as if they had missed the direction from which they had come up. They turned this way and that and could not get away from the ice; it was as if they were clasped in it. They worked down and came to more ice. Finally when the lad went as he thoug⸁t always in the direction from which they had come, t⸱ey came to other deformed fragments but larger and more intimidating for the most part than along the ice-margin, and by crawling and clambering, they managed to get out. At the edge of the moraine were gigantic boulders heaped up in a way the two children had never seen in all their lives. Many were shrouded in white; others on the under sides or where they slanted up had a smooth high-polished surface as if they had been shoved forward on it; some were tilted together like houses or the sides of a roof; some lay one upon the other like misshapen clods. Not far from the children, several were slanted together, and lying on them were great wide slabs like a roof. A little house had thus been formed, open at the front but closed at both sides and the back. It was dry inside since the snow had been falling straight down and not a flake had drifted in.

The children were thankful not to be in the midst of ice any longer but to be standing on solid ground again.

By this time it had grown very dark.

"Sanna," said the lad, "we cannot go down any farther because it's night, and we might fall, or even stumble into a crevasse. Let's go in under the stones where it's so dry and warm, and wait there. The sun will come up again and then we'll run down the mountain. Don't cry, please don't cry, you can have all the things to eat that Grandmother gave us to bring along."

She did not cry. But when they had both gone in under the projecting stone roof where there was even room to

sit, stand or walk about, she sat down close to him and was still as a mouse.

"Mother is not going to be displeased with us," said Conrad. "We shall tell her all about the heavy snow that has kept us and she won't say anything; neither will Father. If we are cold, remember, slap your body with your hands the way the foresters do, and then you'll feel warmer."

"Yes, Conrad," said the little thing.

Sanna was not downcast at not being able to go down the mountain and run home, as he might have expected, for the severe strain—the children had not realized how heavy it was—made it seem good to sit down, inexpressibly good, and they gladly gave in to their weariness.

But now hunger too made itself felt. At almost the same instant, they took out their pieces of bread and ate them. They ate the other things too, bits of cake, almonds and nuts and little things their grandmother had slipped into their pockets.

"Now, Sanna, we must get the snow off us," said the lad, "so we'll not be wet."

"Yes, Conrad," answered Sanna.

They went out in front of their little house, and Conrad first got the snow off his sister. He shook her things by the corners, removed his hat that he had put on her and emptied it of snow and brushed off with a kerchief the snow that was left. Then he got off, as best he could, the snow collected on himself.

It had stopped snowing altogether by this time.

The children felt not a flake.

They went back into the stone house and sat down. Getting up had shown them how tired they really were, and they readily sat down again. Conrad took off his calfskin bag. He got out the cloth that had been wrapped by his grandmother around the cardboard box and paper-covered packages, and laid it about his shoulders for more warmth. He also took the two rolls from the bag and gave them to Sanna. The child ate eagerly,—one and then part of the second. But the rest she gave back to Conrad when she saw that he was not eating. He took it and ate it.

Then both sat and gazed straight ahead.

As far as they could see in the dusk, glimmering snow lay upon everything, separate tiny facets scintillating curiously here and there as if, after absorbing the light all day, they were now reflecting it again.

Darkness fell with the suddenness usual in high altitudes. Soon it was dark all around; only the snow continued to shine with its pallid glimmer. Not only had it stopped snowing but the obscuring mist had begun to lift and was parting here and there, for the children caught the twinkle of a little star. Since the snow shed an actual radiance, as it were, and a veil no longer hung from the clouds, they could see from their refuge the mounds of snow sharply silhouetted against the sombre sky. As it was much warmer in the hut than it had been elsewhere, they rested huddling close against each other, and even forgot to be afraid of the dark. Soon the stars came out in greater numbers, one here, one there, until it seemed not a cloud was left in the sky.

It was the moment when people in the valleys were lighting candles. At first but one is lit and placed on the table to light the room, or just a pine-splinter or a fire in the hearth, and a brightness from all the windows where the family is gathered shines out into the snowy night—but on this evening above all—Holy Night—there would be many more lights to shine upon the presents lying spread on tables for the children, or hanging from Christmas trees; countless numbers would be lit, since in every house, every cot, every room, there were one or more children for whom the Christ-child would have brought something on which the candles must shine. The lad had expected they would soon be down off the mountain, yet of all the many lights in the valley that night, not a candle-beam made its way up to them; they looked out upon nothingness, the blankness of the snow, the sombre sky; everything else was lost in impenetrable distance. At this hour, in all the valleys, children were receiving gifts from the Christ-child; only these two sat alone by the glacier; and the finest gifts they might have received were lying in little sealed packages in the calfskin bag at the back of their shelter.

The cloudbanks had dropped behind the mountains on every side and bending low about the children, the arch of heaven was an even blue, so dark it was almost black, spangled with stars blazing in countless array, and through their midst a broad luminous band was woven, pale as milk, which the children had indeed seen from the valley, but never before so distinctly. The night was progressing. The children did not know that the stars move

westward and on, otherwise it might have been possible for them to tell the hour of night, as new stars appeared and others vanished; they, however, supposed them to be the same ones. The ground all about lay bright in the starlight but they saw no valley, nothing familiar; nothing

69

was to be seen anywhere but whiteness—all was pure white. Only a sombre horn, a sombre head, a sombre arm, was discernible, looming up at this point or that from the shimmering waste. The moon was nowhere to be seen; perhaps it had gone down early with the sun or not risen at all.

After a great while Conrad said: "Sanna, you mustn't go to sleep; you know what Father said, 'if you fall asleep in the mountains you're sure to freeze,' the way the old ash-woodsman went to sleep and was dead on a stone four long months and not a soul knew where he was."

"No, I'll not go to sleep," the little thing answered wearily.

Conrad had shaken her by the hem of her frock to rouse her and make her listen.

Then silence again.

Presently the lad was conscious of a gentle pressure on his arm, that grew heavier and heavier. Sanna had fallen asleep and settled down on him.

"Sanna, don't go to sleep, please don't," he said.

"No," she murmured drowsily. "I'm not asleep."

He moved a little away from her to rouse her, but she just dropped over and would have gone on sleeping on the ground. He grasped her shoulder and shook her. Although his motions were somewhat brisker he found he was cold and that his arm was numb. He was alarmed and jumped up. He clutched his sister, shook her harder

and said: "Sanna, let's stand up a while, so we'll feel better."

"I'm not cold, Conrad," she answered.

"Yes you are, Sanna; get up," he exclaimed.

"This fur jacket is nice and warm," she said.

"I'll help you up," he said.

"No," she said and was silent again.

Then suddenly it came back to him. Grandmother had said, "Just a tiny sip warms the stomach, so that even on the coldest winter day you can't feel the cold."

He picked up the calfskin bag, opened it and groped about till he had found the little flask in which his grandmother was sending his mother the black coffee extract, took the wrappings off, and with considerable effort pulled out the cork. Then he leaned down over Sanna and said: "Here is the coffee Grandmother is sending Mother, taste just a little, it will make you warm. Mother would give it to us if only she knew what we need it for."

The child—who only wanted to rest—said: "I am not cold."

"Just a little, then you may go to sleep."

This prospect tempted Sanna; she so nerved herself for the effort that she almost choked on the liquid. After her, Conrad too drank a little. The double distilled strength of the decoction had an immediate effect, all the more powerful because the children had not tasted coffee before. Instead of going to sleep, Sanna became more

73

animated, and herself admitted that she was cold, but said she felt quite warm inside now, and that her hands and feet were getting warm too. The children even chatted together a while.

As soon as the effect began to wear off, they took more and more of the extract in spite of the bitter taste, and their young nerves, unaccustomed to the stimulant, were strung to a pitch of excitement sufficient to overcome the dangerous drowsiness.

It was midnight by this time. Young as they were, they had always fallen asleep each Christmas Eve when it grew late, under the positive strain of joy and overcome by bodily weariness, had never heard the peal of the bells nor the organ at midnight Mass although they lived close by the church. At this very moment all the bells were ringing, the bells in Millsdorf, the bells in Gschaid, and on the farther side of the mountain there was still another little church whose three clear-chiming bells were ringing out. In remote places beyond the valley there were innumerable churches with bells all ringing at this very hour; from village to village, the waves of sound were floating, and in one village you could at times hear through the leafless branches the chiming of the bells in another. Away up by the ice, however, not a sound reached the children; nothing, for here nothing was being heralded. Along the winding paths of the mountain-slopes lantern lights were moving, and on many a farmstead the great bell was rousing the farm-hands,—unseen here, and unheard. Only the stars twinkled and shone steadily down.

Even though Conrad kept before his mind's eye the fate of the frozen woodsman—even though the children had drunk all the black coffee in the little vial to keep their blood stirring, the reaction of fatigue would have been too much for them and they would never have been able to fight off sleep, whose seductiveness invariably gets the better of reason, had not Nature in all her grandeur befriended them and aroused in them a power strong enough to withstand it.

In the vast stillness which prevailed, a stillness in which not a snow-crystal seemed to stir, three times they heard the roar of the ice. What appears the most inert and is yet the most active and living of things, the glacier, had made the sounds. Three times they heard behind them the thundering as awesome as if the earth had broken asunder, a boom that reverberated through the ice in all directions and, as it seemed, through every smallest vein of it. The children sat, open-eyed, gazing up at the stars. Something now began to happen, as they watched. While they sat thus, a faint light bloomed amid the stars, describing upon the heavens a delicate arc. The faint green luminescence traveled slowly downward. But the arc grew brighter and brighter until the stars paled away while a shudder of light, invading other parts of the firmament—taking on an emerald tinge—vibrated and flooded the stellar spaces. Then from the highest point of the arc sheaves radiated like points of a crown, all aglow. Adjacent horizons caught the brightening flush; it flickered and spread in faint quivers through the vastness round about. Whether or not the electricity in the atmosphere had become so charged by the tremendous snowfall that it flashed forth in these silent magnificent shafts of light, or whether unfathomable Nature was to be explained in some other way: after a while the brightness paled, grew fainter and fainter, the sheaves dying down first, until imperceptible finally, and again there was nothing to be seen in the sky but thousands and thousands of familiar stars.

The children said not a word, the one to the other. They remained, on and on, never stirring from where they sat, gazing intently at the sky.

Nothing particular happened after that. The stars sparkled and fluctuated, crossed now and again by a shooting star.

At last, after the stars had been shining a great while and not even a glint of the moon had appeared, everything changed. The sky grew paler, then slowly but unmistakably it began to color, the fainter stars waned, and there were fewer of the bright ones. Finally the most brilliant had set, and the snow toward the heights could be seen more distinctly. Then one horizon took on a yel-

low tinge, and along its edge a ribbon of cloud kindled to a glowing thread. Everything grew clear, and the distant snow-mounds stood out sharp in the frosty air.

"Sanna, it's almost day," said the lad.

"Yes, Conrad," answered the little one.

"When it's just a bit brighter, we shall leave the cave and run down off the mountain."

It grew brighter and there was not a star to be seen in the sky, and every object stood out clear in the daylight.

"Well, let's be going," said the lad.

"Yes, let's go," answered Sanna.

They stood up and tried their legs which only now felt very tired. Although they had not been asleep all night long, they felt refreshed by the morning. The lad slung the calfskin pouch over his shoulder and drew Sanna's little fur jacket closer about her. Then he led her out of their stony retreat.

Since they thought they would only have to run down off the mountain they gave no thought to food and did not explore the pouch for bits of bread or anything else that might be left.

The sky being clear, Conrad thought he would look down into the valley, recognize Gschaid and climb down to it. But he saw no valley. They did not seem to be standing on a mountain from which one looks down, but rather on strange foreign ground full of unfamiliar sights. Today they saw towering up out of the snow great fearsome rocks in the distance, where they had not seen them the day before; they saw the glacier, snowy hills and slopes standing out boldly, and beyond them, sky or the blue

peak of some distant mountain above the snow-line. At this moment the sun came up.

A gigantic blood-red disc climbed the heavens above the sky-line and at the same instant the snow all around flushed as though bestrewn with thousands of roses. Summits and horns cast long faint greenish shadows across the snowfields.

"Sanna, let's keep on till we get to the side of the mountain and can look down," said the lad.

They now started off through the snow. During the clear night it had become even drier and was easier to walk on. They ploughed along briskly, their limbs becoming supple and strong as they went. But they came to no mountain-side, and could not look down. Snowfield followed snowfield, and always, on the horizon of each, the sky.

Nevertheless they went on.

Then they found themselves on ice again. They did not know how the ice could have got there but they felt the hard glaze underfoot and, although there was no such intimidating wreckage of mighty fragments as on the edge of the moraine where they had spent the night, yet they saw they were treading on solid ice. Now and again they saw blocks of it, more and more of them, still nearer, and these forced them to do more clambering.

Still they kept on, in the same direction.

Now they surmounted monstrous debris; now found themselves again on the icefield. Today in the bright sun, they were able for the first time to see what it was like. In size it was stupendous, and beyond towered yet more sombre rocks; wave after wave heaved up, as it were, and the snow-covered ice, compressed and buckling, seemed to be pushing down upon the children and threatening to flow over their very bodies. In the whiteness they saw countless meandering bluish lines. Between where ice-blocks stood up as if hurled together, there were straight lines like paths, but they were white, with solid ice beneath, where the ice-blocks had not been forced up by intense pressure. The children kept on these paths since they wished to cross at least part of the glacier so as to reach the side of the mountain and be able to look down at last. They spoke not a word. The little one followed her brother. But again today, there was ice, nothing but ice. Where they had meant to cross it stretched on endlessly, farther and farther. Then they gave up and turned back. Where they could not set foot they crept forward on hands and knees along snow-banks that fell in before their very eyes and showed the dark blue of a crevasse— where just before all had been white; but paying no heed they struggled on till they had again come out of the ice.

"Sanna," said the lad, "we're not going out there on the ice again because we get nowhere on it. And since we can't see down into our valley anyhow, let's go down the mountain in a straight line. We are bound to come into some valley, and shall tell the people we are from Gschaid: they will send a guide with us to show us our way home."

"Yes, Conrad," said the little one.

They started down through the snow in the direction

82

that seemed most promising. The young lad took his sister by the hand. However when they had worked down for a time the slopes changed level and began to rise. The children therefore altered their course and crept along a sort of gulley. But it only led them to the ice again. So they clambered up the side of the gulley to find a descent in some other direction. This brought them to a level stretch that by and by however became so steep they could hardly find a foothold and were afraid of sliding down. After climbing through snow a great while and walking along an even ridge, it was again as before, either the slope was so steep they would have lost their footing, or it went on up so far they feared it would bring them to the mountain-top.

They now hoped to find the path by which they had first come up, and make their way back to the red memorial post. Since it was not snowing and the sky was so bright, Conrad thought, they would easily recognize the place where the post ought to be, and then be able to find the way down to Gschaid.

He explained the plan to his sister and she followed him.

But the way to the col was not to be found either.

Shone the sun ever so bright, towered the heights ever so fair above the snowfields, there was no telling the place by which they had made their way up on the previous day. Then all had been so veiled by the terrifying snowfall they had scarcely been able to see a step ahead and everything was an intermingling of white and gray. Only the rocks beside and between which they passed had been visible. Today, too, they had seen many rocks but all of them had looked just like the others. Today they left fresh footprints in the snow but yesterday's had been all covered by the snow as it fell; they could not just by the look of things tell which way led to the col, for all places looked alike. Snow, nothing but snow. But still hoping, they pressed on. They avoided precipitous descents and did not climb any more steep gradients.

Today too they often stood and listened. But now, as yesterday, could hear nothing, not the faintest sound. Again, nothing to be seen but snow; the white white snow, with sombre horns and blackened ribs standing out in bold relief.

At length the lad thought he saw a fire. It seemed to him at last that on a far distant precipitous snowfield a flame was leaping up. It disappeared, went up and died down. Now they saw it, now lost it. They stood and watched fixedly in that direction. The flame kept on leaping and seemed to be coming closer, for they saw it grow larger and saw its flaming more distinctly. It did not disappear so often now or for so long a time. Afterwhile they heard faintly, very faintly, across the still blue distance, something like the long-sustained note of an alpenhorn. Instinctively both shouted with all their might.

Afterwhile they heard the sound again and shouted again, staying where they were. The flame too was coming nearer. They caught the sound a third time, and this time more clearly. They answered again, with a loud shout. After considerable time they recognized the flame. It was not a flame. It was a red flag being waved. Meanwhile the horn sounded nearer, and again they answered.

"Sanna," exclaimed the lad, "people from Gschaid are coming. I know the flag. It is the red flag the foreign gentleman who climbed Gars with the young ash-woodsman planted on top as a signal so the Reverend Father might see it with his spyglass and know they had reached the summit, the flag the foreign gentleman gave the Reverend Father afterward as a present. You were still very little then."

"Yes, Conrad."

Afterwhile they saw people, too, around the flag, little black dots that seemed to be moving about. The call of the horn was repeated from time to time, steadily nearer. Each time the children would answer. Finally they saw several men coasting down the snowy slope on their *alpenstocks,* the flag in their midst. As they came nearer, the children recognized them. It was herdsman Philip with his horn, his two sons, the young ash-woodsman, and several men from Gschaid.

"Praised be God!" cried Philip, "there you are. We are scattered all over the mountain. Someone run down to the upland meadow and ring the bell so they will know we have found them; and someone get out on top of Crab Rock and set the flag up so they can see it from the valley and fire the mortars, to let the people searching Millsdorf forest know; and have them build smudge-fires that will smoke away up high to direct everyone on the mountain to the Sideralp. What a Christmas!"

"I'll run down to the meadow," said one.

"I'll go up on Crab Rock with the flag," said another.

"And we shall bring the children down to the Sideralp as best we may; pray God," said Philip.

One of his sons struck off down hill and the other set out through the snow with the flag.

The young ash-woodsman took Sanna by the hand and herdsman Philip, the lad; the others helping as best they could. Thus they started on their way. It had many a turning, now in this direction, now that. Now up, now down. Always through snow, always through snow they went, the look of the mountainside never changing. For the steepest inclines they fastened spikes to their shoes, and carried the children. At last, after a great while, the tones of a little bell traveled up to them faint and clear,—the first message to reach them from below. They had by this time, in fact, come down a long way, for as they looked, a snow-capped peak soared above them, lofty and blue. The little bell they had heard was the one being rung on

86

the upland meadow, which had been agreed upon as meeting place. When they had come farther down, they also heard, faintly through the still air, the booming of the mortars fired after the flag was hoisted, and later they saw columns of smoke rising tall and thin.

After a time, descending a gentle slope they caught sight of the alpine hut. They walked toward it. Within, a fire was burning, the children's mother was there, and when she saw the children coming with the young ash-woodsman, with a heart-rending cry she sank, faint, on the snow. Then she rushed to them, devoured them with her eyes, wanted to give them something to eat, wanted to make them warm, wanted them to lie down and rest on the hay, but soon satisfied herself that happiness had given them more strength than she had supposed. They needed only the warm food awaiting them; and rest, which also was afforded them.

Presently, the children, after resting a little, ran out with the others to see who was coming, as a second group neared the hut, down through the snow while the little bell kept on ringing. It was the shoemaker, the former mountaineer with his *alpenstock* and spiked shoes, accompanied by friends and fellow craftsmen.

"Sebastian, they are here," cried his wife.

Speechless and trembling, he ran toward them. His lips moved as if to say something but no words came, he pressed the children to his heart, holding them close and long. Then he turned to his wife and locked her in his arms, crying, "Sanna, Sanna."

After a time he picked up his hat, fallen unnoticed on the snow, went over to the group of men intending to speak to them, but could only say: "Neighbors, friends, I thank you."

88

After waiting for a while until the children had had time to recover somewhat from their excitement, he said: "If we are all back now, let us start—and God be with us."

"Not quite all, I believe," said herdsman Philip, "but those who are missing can tell by the smoke that we've found the children, and will go home when they do not find anyone in the hut."

Then everyone got ready to start.

The alpine hut was not far from Gschaid and in summer one could see it plainly from the village with its little bell-tower on the green of the upland pasture; but just below was a precipitous drop of many fathoms; it could be descended in summer but only with spiked shoes, and in winter not at all. One had to take a roundabout way to the col and thence down to Gschaid from the memorial post. By that way, one crossed the alpine meadow which is still nearer Gschaid and could, from there, almost imagine one saw the windows of the village.

Because of the commotion in Gschaid that morning, the priest had postponed High Mass, supposing the children would soon be found. But still no word came, so the rites had to be observed, and when those crossing the Sider meadow heard the little bell that signified the Elevation of the Host, all sank on their knees in the snow and prayed. Then, when the sound of the bell died away, they rose and went on.

89

The shoemaker carried little Sanna most of the way, she telling him everything.

When they had almost reached the col-forest they came upon footprints and the shoemaker said, "No work of mine ever made those marks."

It was soon explained. Attracted, no doubt, by the echoing of the many voices, another searching party was coming to join the one descending. It was headed by the dyer, chalk-white with fear, who had come down the mountain with his workmen, apprentices, and others from Millsdorf.

"They've been over the glacier and the crevasses without knowing it," the shoemaker called out to his father-in-law.

"Well here they are—here they are—thank God," answered the dyer. "I knew they must be up there when your messenger came in the night and we set out with lanterns and searched the whole woodland without finding anything; then as the gray of dawn broke, I noticed on the way from the memorial post, on the left up toward snow-mountain, just where you leave the post, fir-tips snapped off here and there—you know how children like to pull at things as they go along—then I knew they would never be able to get back for they would follow the trench and have the rocks on each side and get up on the ridge that has the sheer drop, and wouldn't be able to get down—would just have to go on up. When I saw that,

I sent word at once to Gschaid. But when woodcutter Michael, who went for me, came back and rejoined us up near the ice, he told us you had found them, so we came down again."

"Yes," said Michael, "I knew it because from Gschaid they'd seen the red flag on Crab Rock which was the signal. And I knew they would all come down this way since you can't come down the bluff."

"Upon your knees, thank God upon your knees, son-in-law," continued the dyer, "that there was no wind. Another hundred years and there may never be another tremendous snowfall like that, coming down straight like wet warp on a pole. If there had been wind, the children would have been lost."

"Ah, thanks be to God, thanks be to God," replied the shoemaker.

The dyer, who had never been in Gschaid since the marriage of his daughter, decided to accompany them all to the village.

When they drew near the red post where the timber-road began, a sleigh which the shoemaker had ordered on the chance of finding the children was waiting. Mother and children were helped in, well covered with rugs and furs already in the sleigh, and sent ahead to Gschaid.

The others followed, and reached the village by afternoon. Those still up on the mountain who had only learned by the smoke that they might turn back, arrived one by one. The last to appear, and not until evening, was herdsman Philip's son who had gone up Crab Rock with the red flag and planted it there.

The children's grandmother who had driven over from Millsdorf, was waiting in Gschaid.

"Never, never as long as they live," she declared, "shall the children be allowed to cross the col in winter."

The children themselves were bewildered by all the commotion. They had been given something to eat and put to bed. Late in the evening when they had somewhat recovered, and while neighbors and friends were congregated in the larger room talking about the events of the day, and in the little room adjoining Sanna's mother was sitting by the bed caressing her, the child said: "Mother, last night when we were up there on the mountain, I saw the Holy Christ-child."

"O my brave long-suffering, my precious, my beloved child," answered her mother, "He has also sent you some presents that you are going to receive now."

The cardboard boxes had been unpacked and the candles lit, the door into the big room was opened, and from their beds the children saw the belated, brightly shining, welcoming Christmas tree. Despite their fatigue they wanted to put on some clothes so that they could go into the other room; and there they received their presents, admired them, and then fell asleep over them.

Gschaid Inn that evening was livelier than usual. All

who had not been in church were there; the others also.
Each related what he had seen and heard, what he had
done, what advised, what he had experienced and all the

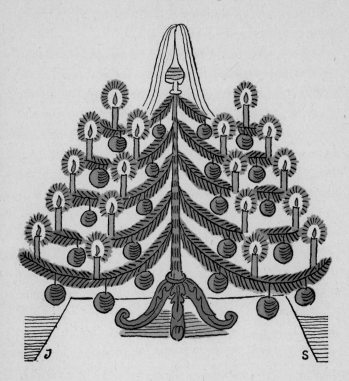

risks he had run. And especially was it emphasized how
everything could have been done differently and better.

The event was epoch-making in the history of Gschaid,
the subject of conversation for a long time, and will be
talked of for years to come, especially on clear days when

the mountain is unusually distinct or when someone is describing its characteristics to strangers.

Only from that day on were the children really felt to belong to the village, and not to be outsiders. Thenceforth they were regarded as natives whom the people had brought back to themselves from the mountain.

Their mother Sanna was now a native of Gschaid too.

The children, however, can never forget the mountain, and earnestly fix their gaze upon it when in the garden, when as in times past the sun is out bright and warm, the linden diffuses its fragrance, the bees are humming, and the mountain looks down upon them as serene and blue as the sky above.